The New Girl

To Sylvain.
V. T.

A big thanks to Clément, Élyse, Frédéric, Inès,
and an extra-special thank you to
Thiên-Thanh and his assistant, Arthur,
for his valuable help with colors.
V. T.

Published in 2010 by Windmill Books, LLC
303 Park Avenue South Suite # 1280, New York, NY 10010-3657

Adaptations to North American edition © 2010 Windmill Books
Copyright © 2007 Editions Milan, 300 rue Léon Joulin - 31101 Toulouse Cedex 9, France.

CREDITS:
Author: Amélie Sarn
Illustrator: Virgile Trouillot
A concept by Frédéric Puech and Virgile Trouillot based on an idea from Jean de Loriol.
Copyright © PLaneTnemo
Translation by Terry Teague Meyer

Publisher Cataloging in Publication

Sarn, Amélie
The new girl. – North American ed. / Amélie Sarn ; illustrations by Virgile Trouillot.
p.   cm. – (Groove High)
Summary: When a new student arrives in the middle of the school year and appears to be
working as a spy for the dreaded Miss Nakamura, Dean of Students, she upsets the lives of
the Groove Team.
          ISBN 978-1-60754-536-1 (lib.) – ISBN 978-1-60754-535-4 (pbk.)
ISBN 978-1-60754-537-8 (6-pack)
          1. Dance schools—Juvenile fiction   2. Boarding schools—Juvenile fiction   3.
Dancers—Juvenile fiction   [1. Dance schools—Fiction
2. Boarding schools—Fiction   3. Dancers—Fiction   4. Jealousy—Fiction]
I. Trouillot, Virgile   II. Title   III. Series
          [Fic]—dc22

Manufactured in the United States of America

Groove High

Amélie Sarn

The New Girl

Illustrations by Virgile Trouillot

Skyview Books

an imprint of
WINDMILL BOOKS™
New York

Me: I'm Zoe. I'm 14 years old, and I'm living my dream: going to Groove High to become a choreographer!

Vic: Vic is my best friend. She's beautiful, blond, and always in high fashion. She is totally fun!

Lena: Lena is too cool. She's an athlete and a rebel. Too bad she can't get herself organized! She always keeps Paco, her chameleon, in her pocket.

Tom: Tom is also super cool. But he's super clumsy. He's got a thing for Vic, who is not interested in him at all.

Table of Contents

Wake-up Call

The door of our room opens with bang.

Tom, breathless, red-faced, hair a mess, runs up the stairs. He's smiling from ear to ear.

"Hey girls, guess what? It's happened! She's here. Miss Berrens went to pick her up and I saw them both in the cafeteria! She is . . ."

"Get out!" Vic shouts, hurling a stuffed animal at his head.

My teddy bear!

Tom backs out the door just in time. Teddy goes splat on the floor.

It's seven-fifteen in the morning. Vic, Lena, and I are still in our pajamas, barely awake.

Vic is clutching her comforter against her chest. She is really steamed. "I can't believe it! Does he think he lives here, or what?"

Lena just laughs.

"You're right about that, Vic. Tom is so used to hanging out in our room that he thinks he doesn't even have to knock!"

"Well, I don't like it!" Vic grumbles, getting up and heading for the bathroom.

Vic is always a little high-maintenance. Except for Lena and me, her roommates, no one sees her before she's completed dressed and ready for her public—hair just right and a touch of makeup. That's the way she is.

We hear her lock the door. Three seconds later, the shower starts.

Lena gives me a puzzled look. She's got Paco, her chameleon, on her knees. I guess she slept with him on her bed.

"What do you think, Zoe?" Lena asks. "Do we let Tom in?"

I shrug. "Sure."

Tom is still just outside our door. He hasn't moved an inch. His face is just as red as before but a sheepish look has replaced his smile.

"I am *soooo* sorry," he says, and we all know he

means it.

"It's okay, come in," Lena says. "If Nakamura catches you she'll hang you up by your heels for sure!"

Tom comes in.

Lena is right, if Nakamura, our Dean of Students, catches a boy in the girls' dorm, he's in major trouble. They don't call her the Dragon or Nakamura the Eel for nothing.

The Eel. Luke Vandenberg came up with that name. Luke is a real whiz with nicknames.

He's a third-year student. I'm not always sure what to make of him, but recently he said something to me that I'll tell you about later . . .

But back to the

present—Tom, that is.

No more running water in the bathroom. Vic must be performing her tooth-brushing ritual.

Tom drops into my chair and starts talking. He's really hyper.

"She is really pretty. Tall, with long dark hair and green eyes. I think they're green. I was sort of far away, so I'm just guessing . . ."

I interrupt him. "Wait a sec. Who in the world are you talking about?"

Tom looks at me like I've lost my marbles. "Duh! The new girl!" He obviously thinks everyone is just like him—completely preoccupied with some new student first thing in the morning.

Then, I remember. The new girl! Khan told us about her at the end of theater class on Friday. He said a new student would arrive today and asked us to be really nice to her because it's so hard to start out in the middle of the school year. He also mentioned that she's extremely talented and a real expert in yoga. (Khan is our yoga instructor.) That alone really annoyed me. Khan is my favorite teacher—he's just great . . . and totally handsome! Up until now *I* was the star in yoga class. I definitely do not want to drop to second-best!

But after the weekend came and went, I completely forgot about her. Actually, the last couple of days Lena and I took advantage of the fact that Vic was out of our room babysitting to talk about . . . well, I'll be discussing *that* later.

Tom, on the other hand, seems to have been thinking about nothing *but* the new girl.

"I got up really early this morning," he says. "I hid behind that humongous plant in the main hall and waited. And waited. I was afraid I'd missed them. And then, there she was! She looks really nice."

"We'll see," Lena says, absent-mindedly petting Paco. "First you say she's really pretty, then really nice. So which do you like more, her smile or her supermodel appearance?"

Tom blushes. That's Tom. He blushes at the drop of a hat.

He stammers, "Well, I don't know . . . she's really pretty and she also seems really nice. Why can't it be both?"

Lena raises an eyebrow, looking unconvinced.

"Humph. We know what you guys really care about. If she wasn't so good-looking, you probably wouldn't think she seemed so nice."

"Hey, that's not true!" Tom protests.

I feel like sticking up for him, but at the same time, I completely agree with Lena. What's the big idea with waking us up with this big story about another girl? And how he could tell how nice she is just by spying on her from behind a plant!

"I'm coming out!" Vic's voice announces from behind the bathroom door.

She comes out as if she's making a center-stage entrance. As usual, she looks perfect. Her long blond hair hangs free. A touch of turquoise eye shadow brings out her blue eyes, and her lips shine with a perfect gloss. She's wearing a jacket that matches her eye shadow and has chosen a really cute layered skirt. Tom stares at her, amazed. His tongue is practically hanging out!

The thing about Tom and Vic is a little weird. We all know it was love at first sight for him. But the poor boy doesn't stand a chance with her. Vic likes older guys. Not only that. She is interested in really classy, popular boys. Tom, who is only thirteen, a year younger than Vic, has crazy-looking hair and freckles. He is definitely way below her standards.

But that doesn't discourage him. He spends all his time doing anything he can for Vic. In return, she either treats him like her servant or ignores him completely!

"Well," Vic announces. "I'm ready. Shall we go?"

Lena and I exchange a look of despair. We've got exactly ten minutes to get ready or we'll be late for breakfast!

And we can't forget to put Paco back in his terrarium.

Bruised Ankle, Wounded Pride

All the way to the cafeteria Tom talks about the new girl, completely ignoring Vic's loud, irritated sighs.

Finally, she leans over to me. "I'm getting sick of hearing about the new girl," she mutters. "What's so special about her?"

I totally agree with Vic. I'm already tired of it myself. Then I point out that there's a positive side to the situation. I whisper to her. "Is it all so bad? Think about it, Vic. Maybe now he'll stop making such a fuss over you. You're always complaining that he never leaves you alone."

"Right!" Vic says sarcastically.

What a morning! And another thing. It doesn't seem right that Ed's not here in the cafeteria as usual.

Oh yes, I haven't told you about him yet. Ed is the fifth member of the Groove Team. The other members are Vic, Lena, Tom, and me. You have to understand—the Groove Team isn't just any old group! We may not agree on everything, but we stick together, and we always watch one another's backs. On top of that, we're the ones who publish *Groove Zine*, an indie magazine that's a big hit at Groove High.

But right now—and this is unusual—Ed isn't here. He got special permission from the school administration to go see his mother dance at the Grand Theater in Mexico City. Ed doesn't have many opportunities to spend time with his mother. She and Ed's father have been divorced for years and since she's a world-famous dancer, she spends her time jetting around the globe. On a whim, she sent Ed plane tickets to join her for this performance. He won't be back until next week.

We sit down at a table. Tom is twisting around in his chair, looking everywhere to spot the new girl. The other girls and I are also looking around, but much more discreetly. As usual, Luke and Zach are sitting in the back of the cafeteria. Lena waves at

Zach who gives her a big smile back.

Zach is one of the top subjects Lena and I spent so much time talking about this past weekend. The other main subject is Luke. But I try hard to not look at him.

Because if I do, I know I'll blush red as a tomato. All of a sudden, Tom is jabbing me with his elbow.

"There she is! Look, that's her!"

Lena, Vic, and I spin around to look toward the door. Yes, there she is. And Tom's description didn't do her justice. The new girl is not just pretty. She is beautiful! Tall, slim, beautiful features, and cascades of silky black hair. Her skin is perfect and she has lovely, slanted green eyes.

She strides in sending out vibes of self-assurance and class. The whole cafeteria is hushed.

Two tables over from us, Kim is gritting her teeth. Kim, who is our sworn enemy! She spends her time putting on this "I'm-the-perfect-student" act for school administrators. Mainly, she tries to get us in trouble! Angie and Clarisse, her devoted servants, can't hide their admiration for the new girl. They're probably going to invite her to be in their clique.

Suddenly Luke gets up, walks over to the new girl, smiles, and sticks out his hand. "Hi, I'm Luke. I'm a third year. If you'd like, you can come and sit with my friend Zach and me . . ."

I've got a huge lump in my throat. I was so involved in my story—what Lena and I were discussing this weekend (and I really will talk about that later)—I had almost forgotten to say that Luke is Kim's brother. He's also known as Luke Dreamboat Vandenberg, and he's a huge flirt.

A gorgeous smile lights up the new girl's face and makes her green eyes positively twinkle.

"Hello, Luke," she says. "Khan already told me

about you. You're head of the Capoeira Club, right? I think that's so cool!" And just like that, she follows Luke and sits down at his table.

I don't want to see or hear any more. I concentrate on my hot chocolate. Little by little, conversation picks up in the cafeteria, but curious students keep looking toward the table in back.

Her name is Yumiko. Everyone's talking about her. As Khan told us, she's a first year, so she's in our class.

While we're hanging out in the courtyard under the watchful eye of Nakamura, Tom goes to talk

to her. Vic, Lena, and I stay back. For some strange reason, the arrival of this new student has created an air of tension you can almost cut with a knife. I'm in a really bad mood, and Vic and Lena are acting the same way.

Our first class today is physical education. Lately we've been working on wushu. It's a martial art that teaches us how to conserve our energy. Our instructor, Mr. Tian, is a two-time world champion, and you don't kid around in his class. He warned us on the first day.

"I don't want anyone lagging behind," he announced in a stern voice. "You must salute your opponent, low blows are forbidden, and your form must always be flawless!"

Of course, Vic, the fashion queen, had to whisper that perfect form was impossible while wearing baggy black pants and a ratty white tee shirt.

The teacher gave her a withering look and I was afraid he was going to knock her flat with a good *zhi bai xing*! (That's what they call the stiff, foot-kick in wushu. I found that out later—the hard way.)

"Take your places, everyone," Mr. Tian barks as we walk in the door.

We must not forget to salute our masters (the ancestors who invented wushu), whose photos hang on the wall. We place the palms of our right hands flat against our left clenched fists. I notice the new girl out of the corner of my eye. She can't know this detail. Mr. Tian will be flying off into one of his rages ... But then I see her doing the salute, following the rules of this martial art! Of course, I should have known, Tom must have told her.

"Warm up!" the teacher commands.

We do stretching on the floor, rapid arm circling and jumping in place until Mr. Tian shouts, "*Ting shi!*"

That means "stop" in Chinese. So we freeze.

"Today," he says, "we're going to do combat.

Therefore, I will put you in pairs . . ."

I immediately move toward Vic, and Lena moves toward Tom, but Mr. Tian ignores whomever we prefer as partners. He chooses which students will pair up for matches.

"Miss Victoria Solis, you will fight against Miss Lena Robertson. Miss Zoe Myer, your opponent will be Miss Yumiko Hyori . . ."

Who, me?? I have to fight the new girl? Okay, okay, so long as she doesn't complain if I hurt her a little. It's a fight after all.

"In your places!" Mr. Tian shouts.

I sneak a look at Vic and Lena. I know that Vic hates to fight with Lena, because she thinks Lena, who is a super athlete, is just a bit too rough.

Here I am face-to-face with Yumiko. It's amazing how pretty she is. Vic improves her looks with light makeup. And Kim (who, I hate to admit, is pretty too) always uses a lot. As for this girl, she's all-natural. But I do think her hair is in an odd style for this class. It's in a knot, without pins or barrettes. I doubt it will stay up, especially during the match.

I salute her with the traditional gesture, and she responds the same way. She seems a little intimidated. Her long lashes blink quickly. Of course, I'm not going to be too hard on her. After all, we've already been doing wushu for four weeks and this is her first class . . .

"We begin in *ma bu tan bian*," Mr. Tian orders, hands on his hips.

I get in position: feet planted firmly, legs apart, knees bent, arms extended on both sides of the body, fists tight.

I whisper to Yumiko, "Just do as I do. This is basic combat position. After that, we do a sequence of movements. But don't worry! I won't use real blows. I'll start with a tap using the edge of my hand, and then . . ."

I don't have the time to finish.

"*Kai shi*!" Mr. Tian shouts. That means "start"!

As I'm getting ready to make a gentle thrust at Yumiko, she makes a surprise move and switches her stance. Suddenly, her foot jabs out at my face so fast I don't even have time to dodge the blow. She doesn't actually touch me, but she misses by only a couple of millimeters. I'm so stunned that I'm slow to react, even when she gets into attack position, legs wide, both hands in front and . . .

I don't see it coming and I'm flat on my back!

"Bravo! Great sequence!" Mr. Tian shouts enthusiastically. "Quick, efficient, perfect. Well, perhaps you should have relaxed your shoulders a bit."

Yumiko responds with the ritual salute to the instructor and adds in a quiet voice, "I don't deserve your praise. I have been practicing wushu since I was ten years old and I had an excellent teacher."

What's this? Since she was ten? It's not fair! I made a fool of myself trying to be nice to her, explaining the position and telling her to watch me . . . And she didn't say anything. Did she really want to make me look ridiculous in front of everyone? And on top of everything, her hair stayed perfectly in place!

She turns to me and holds out a hand. "I hope I didn't hurt you," she says.

I'd rather die than have her help me up! I get up on my own and turn my back on her. No, she didn't hurt me. She managed to make me fall gently, so she must have held back on the power of her thrust . . . but my pride is definitely wounded.

"Everyone in place!" Mr. Tian shouts. "Begin again!"

Limping slightly, I head for the benches at the back of the practice room.

"Miss Myer?" Mr. Tian calls out. "Do you have a problem?"

"It's just that, well, I hurt my ankle when I fell and I have dance class after this, so I thought . . ."

Mr. Tian frowns. It's obvious he doesn't believe me, but what can he say? Groove High is a school for dance, not martial arts.

"Very well then, sit down, Miss Myer. But pay attention to the class. I don't want you to miss any of my instruction!"

"Yes, sir."

Vic and Lena both give me encouraging looks, but I barely respond. I am too upset. No doubt about it, the new girl is really getting on my nerves!

"T" for Tom and "T" for Traitor

It's a catastrophe! A major catastrophe!

I thought it was enough with just Kim and her clique, who do their best to make life miserable for us. Now on top of them we have Yumiko!

My girlfriends and I are starting to wonder which one is worse. After all, we were sort of getting used to Kim!

During the wushu class, Mr. Tian just couldn't stop complimenting her. And she would look down every time, like little Miss Modest. But she can't fool us. Yumiko is so full of herself!

In the dressing room, Vic, Lena, and I completely ignored her. Once she even walked over to me and I just turned my back.

When we got out of the dressing room, Tom was waiting for us. I say "for us" because that's usually the way it is. He always is ready to hold the door

29

for Vic. But this time, (you guessed it) he held it for *her*, the new girl! And he started asking her about her wushu technique, how she did such a great job with this or that movement . . . He was so enthralled with the answers she gave in her annoying, whispery voice that he let go of the door and it slammed right in Vic's face!

Just imagine how furious Vic was. She positively screeched, "Tooooom!"

He turned around and immediately realized what he'd done. Of course, he turned a thousand shades of red and rushed over to Vic, apologizing all over the place. But it was too late. The new girl stuck around for about two seconds and went right on ahead.

Vic yelled at Tom for what seemed like forever. I almost felt sorry for him. But at the same time, I was thinking it served him right. He acted like the Groove Team motto "Stay united!" didn't mean anything to him anymore. Instead he dropped us for the first new girl who came by.

"Besides," Vic ranted, "You're making a fool of yourself going after that girl! Don't you see she doesn't care a bit about you? What do you think . . .

she's going to fall for *you*?"

For a moment, I wondered if Vic wasn't a little jealous . . . Maybe? . . . Uh-uh. Not possible. She has absolutely no interest in Tom. Hasn't she told us that constantly? So why would she be jealous?

Tom shouted back at her, "What are you saying? I think she's cool, that's all. And why are you treating her so badly?"

Then that set *me* off. "What?!? We're treating *her* badly? You've got to be kidding. Didn't you see what she did to me in wushu class?"

Tom shrugged. "What? What exactly did she do to you? She's just stronger than you, that's all."

I was totally shocked at his disloyalty.

Vic got in the last word. "Well, Tom, if you think she's so nice, just go catch up with her. We'd love any break from your annoying company."

"But . . ." Tom started to protest.

Vic cut him off with a dirty look. Tom, crestfallen, stayed with us.

Just now we're heading into the dance classroom. I am expecting the new girl to be wearing a fancy low-cut leotard with skinny straps or boy-shorts with a ruffled top like Kim, but no, she has on a basic long-sleeve leotard. Hers is exactly like mine—only orange.

I notice that she's standing off to the side of the room.

"Ladies and gentlemen," Iris Berrens says to welcome us. Mrs. Berrens is director of the school, a former prima ballerina and Groove High's top dance instructor. "Today we are going to devote ourselves to lifts."

Yuck! That is what I hate the most. During a lift, the girl must seem weightless, light as a feather. And, when you see me, I fly more like an elephant!

"As there are few boys in the class," she continues, "they have twice as much work to do! I remind you that the success of a lift depends equally on the one who is lifting and the one being lifted! Sylvan, Tom, Axel, Ed, take your places!"

Lena raises her hand. "Excuse me, Mrs. Berrens. Ed is not here."

Mrs. Berrens raises an eyebrow. "Oh yes, that's right. I'd forgotten! Well then, we'll have to make do without him. You other young men, stand ready! And now girls, line up!"

Vic is the first to be lifted, by Sylvan. She is sublime—no surprise there. She seems to take flight and she makes it look simple.

"Well done, Miss Solis," the teacher comments.

Now it's Yumiko's turn, with Tom lifting. He must be thrilled! Of course, she's perfect as well.

Now it's Lena's turn . . .

Ooops! From the start, I sense that she's going to get it wrong. She doesn't leap high enough. She lands

. . . in Axel's arms, and he collapses under her dead weight. The whole class (except Tom, Vic, and me, of course) bursts out laughing. Kim howls louder than all the others. Yumiko is silent. Good. Otherwise, I think I would have bitten her head off—unless Vic got there first!

When my turn comes, my legs are trembling. I leap up and wow! Success! Sylvan catches me and sets me down on his other side.

"Bravo, Sylvan!" Mrs. Berrens beams. "You almost make us believe that Miss Myer has become graceful

. . .You note the *almost*," she adds, giving me a cold look.

But I really don't mind her remark. When I become a choreographer, I will never put any lifts in my ballets!

Lena elbows me. At the back of the room, Kim has gone over to the new girl. They're talking. Humph! It doesn't surprise me that those two are getting along so well!

"Let's keep at it, young people!" Mrs. Berrens commands, lightly tapping her baton on the floor. "Continue practicing. You will perform lifts until you do them perfectly."

Great! Just what I wanted to hear.

We get back in line. Tom is all set to lift dancers in the same order as before when Vic grabs his elbow. "You are nothing but a traitor," she hisses.

"What?" Tom whispers, obviously surprised. "What makes you say that?"

"You think I didn't notice you helping out the new girl? Without you, she would have been a real flop!"

"That's not true! Her technique was perfect," Tom says—a little too loudly.

Mrs. Berrens taps her baton. "Mr. Muller, you're holding things up!"

As Tom moves to obey the teacher, he turns for a moment and says. "Frankly, I don't get your attitude, Vic! You and Lena and Zoe—you're acting so mean to Yumiko that I'm starting to think you're just plain jealous!"

"Mr. Muller!" Iris Berrens calls out in her haughty tone.

Tom gets back in line. Vic is absolutely furious. So am I! I could never have imagined he'd talk that way to Vic. Or anyone else, really. What happened to the old Tom—our shy, clumsy friend? You know, the one who's lovesick over Vic, and ready to obey her every command just so she'll notice him? We don't recognize this guy. He's suddenly transformed into a knight in shining armor, ready to do battle for his lady. His lady! She's none other than the new girl whom we really don't know and who has managed to enrage Vic, Lena, and me in a few short hours!

Tom, a member of the Groove Team, seems to be forgetting the group's basic principle. "We support each other no matter what!"

Could this girl have cast a spell on him? Sure,

that sounds a little nutty, but I'm trying to consider all the possibilities. Maybe she possesses evil powers . . .

If only Ed were here! Ed would know exactly what to do. He would give Tom a convincing speech about friendship and get Tom back on the right track.

Standing beside Vic, I sense that she's furious. Her shock immediately turns into rage. Fists clenched, she spits out her words, "That traitor!"

That's it! She's described him perfectly! Tom is a traitor.

The Dragon's New Pet

Today at noon, Tom didn't even sit with us at our table. He didn't sit with Yumiko either. She was invited to join Kim and her clones.

So Tom ate by himself in a corner, while we endlessly discussed him and Yumiko. Of course, we didn't completely leave Kim out of the discussion.

I noticed that Vic was having a hard time without Tom around to get her drink refills and take away her trash . . . And Lena was worried about something else. She couldn't get her mind off Zach and Luke, who have disappeared. Of course, she doesn't really care about Luke, but Zach is another story . . .

Okay, it's time to tell all.

A while back, Zach, Luke's best friend—he's another third-year student who's also an officer in the Capoeira Club—asked Lena to go to a basketball game.

Nothing actually happened between them. No kiss, not even handholding . . .

Even so, Vic and I kept begging Lena for details about the date, and after a while Lena just clammed up. Actually, she's always stuck to the same story: Zach is nice, they both like sports, and that's all there's to it!

But this weekend . . . while Vic was away babysitting, Lena and I talked about it endlessly. And she finally

admitted to me that's she's a got a huge crush on Zach!

Um . . . obviously!

But she has no idea how Zach feels. She's afraid he just thinks of her as a kid. After all, he's a third-year student, and she's still in her first year (even though she's actually a year older than Vic and me). She hides all these mixed-up feelings though. Whenever she sees Zach, she gives him a wave and a smile, and he always smiles and waves the same way.

But today, we noticed that Zach has not shown up in the cafeteria for lunch. We didn't hang around in the cafeteria for long.

Outside in the hall, Lena speaks up at last. "I keep wondering where Zach is. I didn't see him at morning break and now he's not around for lunch either!"

"They're training for the capoeira contest that's coming up this weekend," says a soft voice behind us.

We turn around. Yumiko! I look around for Kim, but she's not there. Yumiko is alone. What's she doing there? Is she spying on us or what? And then, how did she know . . .

"How do you know?" Lena bursts out. "How do

you know where they are?"

For a moment, Yumiko seems taken aback by Lena's tone. "Well . . . I . . . they told me themselves, this morning . . . They invited me to watch them in the contest . . ."

Lena is fuming. I'm sure I'll see smoke pouring out of her ears any minute. I grab her arm, signal to Vic, and we head toward the courtyard. We sit down on our usual bench.

"I can't believe this!" Lena says. "This girl arrived only this morning and Zach has already invited her to the capoeira competition. And he hasn't even breathed a word of it to me!"

Vic is furious too. "I always expected Luke to tell me about something like this ahead of time!"

Okay. Now we've come to the second big topic of conversation between Lena and me this weekend.

Here is it in a nutshell: Two weeks ago, Luke told me . . . how can I explain it? He let me know . . . that he likes me a lot. Yeah I know. It's hard to believe. He's the most popular, best-looking guy in school. But that's the way it is! Go figure. His exact words were: "I like charming and natural girls . . . like you!"

If that throws you for a loop, that makes two

of us! But wait, there's more. Since then, Vic told me that she's decided to go out with Luke. She's convinced that Luke likes *her* and she's sure this is the perfect time to let him know she feels the same! She seemed so confident that I didn't dare tell her what he said to me.

Now you see why this is such a big problem!

"So, now that I know there's a capoeira competition," Vic goes on, "I'm definitely going to show up and cheer for him. And after that—I'll go for it."

I turn to her. "What do you mean? What will you do?"

"I'll ask him to go out with me."

I feel my chest tighten. I can't really say how I feel about Luke. Sometimes, I hate him, sometimes I think he's . . . adorable. But one thing is sure, I definitely don't want Vic, my best friend, to go out with him. After all, I'm the one he . . .

"Hey, look!" Lena exclaims.

Yumiko is sitting on a bench across the courtyard, reading a manga. Nakamura is heading toward her. Oh boy, this is going to be interesting. When Nakamura bothers to head your way, it's never a good thing. Could the new girl have disobeyed some major rule without knowing about it?

Nakamura crosses the courtyard stiff as a soldier and stops, hands on hips, in front of Yumiko. The new girl looks up and . . . smiles.

Nakamura crosses her arms, but she doesn't yell. She appears to be talking normally.

The new girl keeps smiling. She

nods her head and begins talking herself. Nakamura is listening to her . . .

It's unbelievable!

Since the beginning of the school year, we've never seen Nakamura do anything except come down hard on students, make sure they follow school rules, and threaten to punish them. She even gets on Jeremy's case. He's Groove High's school custodian and building and grounds supervisor, and sometimes Miss Nakamura assigns him to do things like monitor study halls. She keeps him busy! Jeremy kind of looks, and acts, like a big old teddy bear. Miss Nakamura's always telling him to be tough on students and make sure we're following all the school rules to the letter. He does keep an eye on things, but he always tries to be nice about it. Unlike Miss Nakamura, who seems to have it in for all the students.

Oh, excuse me. I'm exaggerating a bit. Nakamura does have one teacher's pet and she lets her pet get away with anything. It's Kim. Nakamura never raises her voice to Kim. Even so, Kim never sits around having friendly chats with her!

But I'm forgetting a very strange scene I saw a

few weeks ago. I was wandering around in the hall by the dance practice rooms when I heard a sound. I peeked in at the door and found Nakamura the Eel in person, dancing and humming, all alone. Maybe not exactly dancing, but she was in first position, arms in arched over her head and she seemed totally focused. It was unbelievable! I closed the door as quietly as possible and ran off.

When I told the members of the Groove Team about what I had seen, they could hardly believe it. Tom and Lena were sure that I was kidding. Vic said something like "Anyway, you know Nakamura is a little off." Ed was the only one to take my story seriously.

I definitely miss Ed. He always manages to find out interesting info about the teachers at Groove

High. It helps that his father, Philippe Kauffman, the famous choreographer, went to school with Iris Berrens and Khan.

It's over now. Nakamura has walked away and Yumiko is back to reading her manga.

"Did you see that?" Vic asks. "First it's Kim and now Yumiko is the Dragon's latest teacher's pet!"

"No surprise there," Lena grumbles. "One thing for sure, that girl is a snake. Definitely! Did you notice how happy she was to mention she knew what Zach was up to? She's the worst."

Vic and I didn't have to say anything. Lena had pretty well summed up our thoughts.

The bell rings. It's back to class.

Something Shady

Tuesday morning. I'm exhausted. Lena and Vic aren't doing any better. We were up talking almost all night. You probably guessed the main topic: the new girl! Tom didn't show up for class yesterday afternoon. The teachers didn't even ask about him. We figured he must have had a good excuse. But still, we didn't have any idea where he was. Did he get permission to train with the third-year students for the capoeira competition? Probably. And since he was mad at us, he didn't bother to tell us. It's awful. The new girl is tearing the Groove Team apart. I just wish I could make her disappear.

Other than that, nothing much happened all day yesterday. The new girl avoided us. I think she figured out we weren't ready to be her best friends forever. Oddly, she didn't hang out with Kim either. Stranger still, Kim wasn't exactly warming up to

Yumiko. Actually, she seemed to be giving her dirty looks that Yumiko just ignored.

That night, we put our heads together and came up with a plan. It was a devious plan to get back at the new girl! We are definitely going to make her regret that she is has upset our lives in this school!

I was half asleep in yoga class and didn't do much in art class either. Now it's noon. Tom more or less ignored us all morning. He did talk to Yumiko a little—making a fuss over her drawings. What a dork!

We're on our way to the cafeteria as Tom comes up. "Hi, girls," he says shyly. We snub him at first. He deserves it.

"Okay, will you drop the silent treatment? I'm really sorry for what I said yesterday . . ."

"It's a little late to apologize," Vic snaps.

Tom doesn't fight back. He sighs and pleads miserably, "Girls, give me a chance . . ."

I'm starting to feel sorry for him. I reach out and touch his arm. "Okay, you're forgiven. But I hope you realize that you nearly broke up Groove Team."

Tom nods.

Vic turns to him. "We're going to give you a chance to make up for it," she says.

Tom's face lights up. As usual, he's ready to do anything to make Vic happy.

"Here's what you have to do," Vic says. "Spy on the new girl for us."

Tom turns completely red. "What . . . what do you mean?" he stammers.

We decided that spying on the new girl is Step One of a brilliant plan to knock her off her pedestal. First, we'll try to figure out what she really cares about. When we find that out, we'll figure out a way to use it against her!

"Don't act like you don't understand," Vic goes on. "You're going to pretend to be her buddy and then report everything she says and does back to us!"

"But why?"

"Because we're going to teach her a lesson. And

to do that, we have to know exactly how to get to her."

All of a sudden, Tom stares as us as if we're aliens. He looks at Vic, then Lena, then me. He shakes his head. "You're all crazy!"

He says it again. He sounds frantic. "You are completely crazy! Why do you want to be mean to Yumiko? As far as I know, she hasn't done anything to you. She even said she didn't understand why you're treating her this way! In fact, I was just about to make a great suggestion. You could recruit her to help Zoe do drawings for *Groove Zine*! She's really talented and . . ."

"Stop it!" Vic is nearly screaming at him.

Lena and I keep quiet. Tom says we're crazy, but really he's the one who's out of his mind. Imagine including that girl in the *Groove Zine* staff! I'd never let her be in charge of illustrations. That's ridiculous. I'm the group's illustrator. Me and nobody else!

But Tom doesn't back off. Red as a beet, body completely tense, he roars back. "You know who you remind me of? *Kim!* Don't look so shocked! You're acting just as mean and stupid as she does. I'm just sorry Ed's not here so he could straighten you out!"

Then, he turns on his heel and stamps off down the hall.

We sit on our special bench in the courtyard, totally depressed. After all that, I'm almost sure the new girl has some magical power! Tom's not acting like himself. I mean, how could he possibly compare us to Kim?

I look around for him, but he's disappeared. We still don't know where he was yesterday afternoon. Zach and Luke aren't around either. Yumiko is seated in the same place as yesterday, with another manga. She appears to be a big fan. Just like me. Too bad

she's so annoying. It would be fun to trade books with her.

What's wrong with me? Am I losing it? Okay, I need to refocus.

Yumiko closes her book and gets up. She's heading toward the door into the hall . . . where Nakamura seems to be waiting for her. I signal for the other girls to watch.

Yumiko comes up to Nakamura and starts talking. Then she gets out an envelope and hands it to the Dean. Nakamura takes it and slips it into her pocket without even glancing at Yumiko. Yumiko starts talking again . . .

I feel like I'm watching a silent movie.

Nakamura gestures in an irritated way. Yumiko is becoming more insistent. The conversation is heating up. I can't tell if it's still a conversation or if it's become an argument. Suddenly, Nakamura turns around and walks away, stiff as a rod. Yumiko just stands there, hands at her side.

What's going on here? Did the new girl know Nakamura from the past? What about the letter she was holding? Maybe it's a report about other students. That idea crossed my mind before, and now it's starting to make sense. Maybe she's some kind of spy or undercover agent. We are going to have to be super-careful. And poor Tom! He's obviously been completely fooled. Maybe Yumiko has been trying to infiltrate the Groove Team! You know, just like in the movies when undercover police pass as criminals to get more evidence before arresting them.

"We're going to have to stay alert at all times," Lena says. "There is definitely something fishy going on."

"I'm with you," Vic says. "Let's put the intensive spy plan in action right now!"

Spies in Action

"This is Vic reporting on the period between 4:00 and 5:00 p.m.," Vic says. "Subject No. 1 stayed in study hall the whole hour. She either worked or pretended to work. Kim came over to talk to her but their conversation was very brief. Kim returned to her seat, looking really annoyed. After that Subject No. 1 didn't talk to anyone. When the bell rang, she picked up her bags and left. I followed her to the door, then exited also."

Vic is standing in our room. We've transformed it into a virtual command center. Lena has drawn a large chart where we record, hourly, every single movement Yumiko makes. (She is now known as "Subject No. 1.") For the period between 4:00 and 5:00 p.m., she's written NOI in large letters. Nothing of importance.

Subject No. 2 is Nakamura. Lena and I are responsible for watching her movements. Two spies are needed for her, as you can never be sure of where she's going to be. She patrols the entire school, speeding from one area to another. Lena and I have to take turns to keep up with her.

During class time, things get really complicated. Lena and I have to keep coming up with excuses for leaving the room in order to check up on Subject No. 2.

"Lena and Zoe reporting on the period between 4:00 and 5:00 p.m.," Lena says. "We followed Subject No. 2 everywhere. She spent 15 minutes in her office, and then went to the kitchen before knocking on Iris Berrens's office door. She stayed there for a half hour. After the final bell, Zoe saw her return to her small apartment on campus."

I nod my head, indicating I agree with her report. Nakamura, I mean Subject No. 2, has her own apartment on campus—just like Iris Berrens and Khan.

Vic takes a big marker from Lena and writes NOI in the section on the chart for Subject No. 2 between 4:00 and 5:00 p.m.

"I hope you realize that the most difficult part of this spy plan is still ahead of us," Vic says, tossing her long blond hair behind her ear. "We absolutely must not let up on our surveillance. So I'm going to wait outside Yumiko's room and you better get back to your places in the administration wing of the building."

I breathe a nervous sigh. We know it's a big risk to be caught in that wing when all the offices are closed . . . We would be expelled from school! No exceptions to that rule.

"Are you still up for it?" Vic asks.

Lena jumps in. "Of course! What did you think? Did you think Zoe and I would quit?"

I chime in, "Of course, we're in for this! What do you take us for?" I probably don't sound as convincing as Lena (because I'm scared to death), but what else can I say?

"Okay, back to work!" Vic orders.

The halls are carpeted, so our steps are muffled. We finally get to the front of Nakamura's door. We flatten ourselves against the wall. Just to be safe, we don't turn on any lights.

"Look," Lena whispers, "her door is not completely

closed." It's true. A sliver of light shines out one side of the door.

"Maybe she's expecting someone," Lena says.

I shrug. Which is really dumb because Lena can't see me in the dark.

"Hey, this is a great chance to give her a scare. We could kick her door open and . . ."

I interrupt. "No way! What are you thinking? That's not why we're here, in case you forgot. We're just here on surveillance."

"Well then, let's see what's going on inside," Lena says, tiptoeing over to the door.

I try to stop her. "Lena . . ."

Too late!

Lena has pushed on the edge of the door, very gently, without a sound. And since I'm dying of curiosity, I'm right beside her.

I hear humming. It's the same humming as I heard last time in the dance practice room!

Miss Nakamura has her back turned. She's in front of a dressing table. She's unpinning her bun and long, very long, gray hair falls down her back. Just like last time in the practice room. And now she's getting up.

She's wearing an elegant black leotard. She's watching herself in the mirror as she turns around. Without her glasses, I notice she has magnificent green eyes. She's . . . it's hard to describe, no wait, it's unbelievable but I felt the same way last time. She's really beautiful!

And now, she's . . . dancing!

Lena and I are stunned at the sight of her. And I know what Lena is

thinking. She is struck by the same impression that hit me when I saw Nakamura the last time. Vic is never going to believe this!

I jump at the sound of footsteps behind me. I grab Lena's arm and practically throw her against the wall. We hide behind a post in the hallway.

It's Yumiko! She's stopped in front of Nakamura's door, about to knock. She leans forward . . . she must have noticed that the door's ajar. She waits a few moments, hesitating, then she knocks.

"We were right!" Lena whispers in my ear. "Those two are definitely up to something!"

"Who's there?"

We hear Nakamura's dry voice on the other side of the door. Yumiko is shifting nervously from one foot to the other. Then, finally, she answers.

"It's me, Yumiko."

"Wait!"

Yumiko crosses her arms. She seems ready to bolt at any moment, but in a few minutes the door opens. We can see Nakamura wearing a robe. Her hair is back in a bun and she's wearing her glasses. She signals for Yumiko to come in and she disappears into the room.

We stand there, paralyzed. I never imagined our spy mission would turn out like this! Wait till Vic hears about . . .

"Hey, are you there?"

"Vic?" I can barely make out her silhouette in the dark.

"Yes, it's me," she whispers. "I was following Yumiko."

Of course! She was following Yumiko and she ended up at Nakamura's place

because that's where Yumiko went!

"See! I told you there was something strange going on between these two," Vic starts. "We did the right thing by . . ."

But she doesn't finish her sentence. We can hear shouting coming from Nakamura's apartment. Yumiko and the Dean are arguing! This situation is completely wacky! And the new girl isn't being quiet about it. Although we can't make out her words, we know it's definitely her voice.

Before we have time to react, Yumiko rushes out the door and slams it behind her!

Back in our room, we're calling off our intensive spy plan until we figure out what to do next. We've got to analyze this new development. First question: Do we tell Tom or not? We can't agree.

"It's useless," Vic says. "He won't listen to anything bad about her. The dope is in love with that girl!"

"But wait," I say, "now's the perfect time to open his eyes to the truth!"

Vic shakes her head.

"He'll brush us off just like he did this morning."

"It wouldn't hurt to try," Lena offers. "We could . . ."

Knock! Knock! Knock!

Three taps on our door. We look at each other nervously. Who could it possibly be at this time of night?

"Girls!" It's a muffled voice. "Open up! It's me, Tom."

His ears must have been burning . . . I jump up and let him in. We were mad at him when he left us this morning, but we still can't leave him out in the hall! He seems very upset.

"Good timing," Lena says, before he has time to open his mouth. "We were just saying we wanted to see you."

"Me too," Tom bursts out. "I just found out some-thing awful . . . It's about Yumiko . . ."

"We already know everything!" Vic inter-rupts.

Tom's eyes get big as saucers. "You do?"

"Here's the deal," Vic says. "We completed our investigation. We know everything . . . almost. The new girl is a spy for Nakamura. We're sure there's more to their relationship, but we have to investigate more to find those details. But we do know we want to get back at Yumiko and she deserves it!"

"What?" Now Tom's eyes are have grown to the size of dinner plates, if that's possible. He gasps as if the air has been knocked right out of him.

"Get back at her," he cries, shocked. He shakes his head as if he hasn't heard right. "At Yumiko? But that's not it, it's . . ."

"What else?" Vic snaps. "Are you still trying to stick up for her? After what we found out about her?"

"But it's not her fault, you see. Actually, we need to help her! I've . . ."

"Help her!" Vic bursts out. "Help a sneaky spy! Don't you see, Tom, you've been completely fooled! Listen to me and, this time, I'm not joking. Either you're with us and you'll help us make her stop causing trouble, or you can just get out of this room right now!"

Tom looks pleadingly at Lena and me. I'm almost ready to feel sorry for him, until I remember how

Yumiko has blinded him. He admits knowing the truth about her, yet he still is on her side. I refuse to look at him. Lena turns away, too.

Tom walks out, slamming the door behind him.

The Green Prank

I spend a very restless night. Right now, sleeping is impossible. That's bad, because I need to be sharp in the morning. My roommates and I are on an important mission.

Last night, we came up with multiple plans to reveal Yumiko's spying to everyone. We finally hit on a simple but foolproof plan. But this idea is going to take of lot of coordination.

In the cafeteria, we'll wait until Yumiko goes for hot chocolate. We've noticed before that chocolate is her favorite drink at breakfast. Lena will spill it in her lap, so Yumiko will have to go to the ladies' room to clean up. Vic and I will be waiting there to corner her. Then Lena will come in and we'll all pressure Yumiko until she admits what she's really up to. Next we'll put out a special edition of the

Groove Zine to expose her to the entire school. After that, no one will speak to her. She'll never be able to cook up secret schemes again!

So here we are in the cafeteria. I take a deep breath.

She's not here!

We go into the main room. Everyone is already at the tables, eating. The same places in back are empty. You know, the ones where Luke and Zach usually sit. (They've been absent for three whole days now!) Tom is all by himself in the corner, hunched over his cereal. All the first-year students are here except . . . Yumiko.

We sit down without saying anything. We all three face the main entry, so we can be sure not to miss her.

I'm reaching for some jam when Lena murmurs, "Do you think she suspected what we planned?"

Vic shrugs. "That's impossible. We just figured out the plan last night."

Still holding the jam, I whisper, "Yeah, but you're forgetting that she's a spy! If that's true, then she probably has tiny microphones all over the place!"

My friends are speechless. They hadn't thought

of that. We must be up against a professional spy!

Suddenly, I don't want any jam. No bread either. I don't even think I can drink my hot chocolate. Every moment I think Nakamura is going to appear and demand that we stand up in front of everyone. I imagine that she presents all the incriminating evidence against us and announces that we're being kicked out of Groove High!

The bell rings. Breakfast is over and for the time being, no one has caught us in a terrible crime. We go out into the courtyard and when Nakamura stands before us, the first year class, she hardly seems to notice us! Usually, she complains about some tiny rule that we've broken. I do notice she frowns when she discovers Yumiko is absent.

Now we're in the dressing room of the dance classroom. I'm changing out of my sweater as Lena pulls on her tights. Vic pokes me in the ribs.

"This is hysterical!" Vic whispers. "Look! Look, it's really funny!"

Of course, I've got my sweater over my face and I can't seem to pull it up. There! Got it.

Yumiko has just come into the dressing room. She's sitting in a corner. Everyone is sneaking looks at her.

What's going on? If her act is to get everyone in the whole world to notice her, she's succeeding! She's got a scarf wrapped around her head that hides her hair and most of her face. She's turned up the collar of her jacket and put on gloves.

What's the reason for this disguise?

Over on the other side of the room, I see excitement bubbling. Kim, Angie, and Clarisse are howling with laughter. They're even clapping their hands and giving high fives as if they pulled off something big.

Except for them, everyone in the dressing room is quiet. Why is the new girl acting so weird?

"Young ladies," Iris Berrens calls out. "The gentlemen have already finished changing. They're waiting for you!"

We go into the dance classroom. Yumiko follows, head down. Seeing her, Mrs. Berrens raises her eyebrows. Yumiko is heading toward her, when . . .

Clarisse jostles Angie, who grabs Yumiko's scarf! And then, we can see the damage as plain as day.

Yumiko has green hair. On top of that, she has a green face!

Then, I figure out why she's wearing gloves. They must be covering up her hands, which must be— green. A very mean, clever person must have put dye in her shampoo and face cream.

Then all eyes are riveted on her. She bursts into sobs and runs out of the room.

Tom strides over to us, "You're despicable!" he says under his breath. "Worse than Kim." Then he runs off after Yumiko.

A very awkward silence hangs over the practice room. Now even Kim and the two others don't dare break it. Mrs. Berrens's eyes sweep around the room, shooting daggers.

"Who did this?" she demands angrily. "I want the guilty party to come forward immediately."

No sound—not even a breath—can be heard from any of the students. Me? I'm star- ing really hard at the toes

of my ballet slippers.

"I remind you," Mrs. Berrens says sharply, "that Groove High is not only a school where you learn to dance, but also a place where you learn important values. What you become in life depends not only on your talent and effort, but also on the choices you make! You can choose to be courageous or cowardly. You can choose to take responsibility or ignore your duty. You can be respectful of others or self-centered. You can choose to be intelligent or ignorant! So, as long as the guilty party's identity is unknown, I will consider none of you here worthy of my instruction."

I close my eyes. I can still see Tom's look of disgust as he said, "You're despicable!" How could he possibly think that we're responsible for this?

I can guess.

After all, what we were planning to do wasn't much better. I'm suddenly ashamed. I think of Mrs. Berrens's words. I don't want to be self-centered or cowardly or ignorant! I want . . .

Mrs. Berrens raps her baton on the floor.

"Very well, since you persist in keeping silent, you'll all be put in detention. No leaving the school today. You're punished until further notice."

Jeremy, whom Miss Nakamura has put on detention duty today, is really surprised to see us all in detention. I've been assigned the job of writing him a note to explain why we're all here.

"What's going on?" he asks, bewildered, before reading the note. "Mrs. Berrens isn't sick or anything, is she?"

I don't answer. The words just get stuck in my throat.

Jeremy reads the note and heaves a loud sigh.

"Go sit down. And no talking!" he orders us. But then he asks me to wait.

"You've got to know who did this! You and the other Groove Team members."

I shake my head. "No, we don't know anything."

I sit down. Tom has just arrived. He goes to sit down too—as far away from us as possible and without a glance in our direction. Jeremy gets out his manga. The moment he does, everyone starts whispering, obviously trying to figure out who could have pulled off this dirty prank.

Kim, Angie, and Clarisse don't seem to be asking each other many questions. They look perfectly self-satisfied.

"We've got to send a note to Tom," Lena suggests. "He's got to know that we weren't involved in this."

"Right," Vic agrees.

I tear out a page from my sketchpad. "But what should we say?" I ask.

Vic starts dictating immediately: "Tom, you must believe us. We didn't know anything about what happened to Yumiko. We would never, never do anything so low! Also, we're really sorry about what we said to you. You've got to help us find the one who did this. Please, please, come back to the Groove Team! Now, everybody, sign your names."

Vic talks so fast that I can hardly write it all down. Apparently, I'm not the only one to be ashamed of what we were planning.

Mrs. Berrens's words hit home. Of course we still need to solve the mystery of the Yumiko-Nakamura connection, but we'll work on that later!

I wad the paper into a ball and hand it to Lena. Of the three of us, she's got the best aim. After all, she's a basketball champ.

And once again, she scores. The note lands right

in front of Tom. He picks it up and flattens it out gently. Hooray! I was afraid he might throw it away without reading it.

Suddenly, we hear three raps on the door of the detention hall. Jeremy hides his magazine in the drawer before calling out "Come in!"

He's smart to hide the magazine, because you never know who it might be. If Nakamura finds him reading rather than watching us like a hawk, she'll hang him up by the ears.

The door opens. It's Ed! He just stands in the doorway for a moment.

It's impossible! He's supposed to be in Mexico with his mother. He's not due back until next week!

Beware of Free Sushi

"Ed?" Jeremy asks, surprised. "What are you doing here? I thought you were in Mexico!"

Ed shrugs and gives Jeremy an apologetic smile. "I got back earlier than planned. Instead of staying home alone, I thought I'd come here."

He points toward an empty table near the back of the room. "Can sit down over there?"

Jeremy, still baffled, nods his head.

Ed glances over at us. Vic, Lena, and I are on one side of the room and Tom is on the other. He frowns. I blush. Ed left only four days ago, and in that little bit of time, we've managed to tear the Groove Team apart. We're such losers. Ed hesitates and looks around. Lena waves at him and mouths. "What are you doing here?"

"Tell you later," he mouths back.

Then he looks over at Tom, sitting all alone with a

miserable expression. Ed walks to his table.

The girls and I notice they're talking softly. Tom gets excited, waves his hands around, shakes his head, and runs his hands through his hair. His cheeks turn bright red. Ed, calm as always, listens and responds from time to time. Then he puts his hand on Tom's shoulder and gets up. Now he's heading our way.

Jeremy is still absorbed in his magazine. Ed pulls up a chair and sits down next to us.

"I just talked to Tom," he says.

I jump in immediately. I can't stand the thought of Ed thinking I'm . . . we're . . . capable of that horrible prank!

"We're not the ones who did that

to Yumiko, Ed! I promise you!"

Ed nods and looks straight into Vic's eyes.

"Me, too! I'm not lying to you. We would never do such a mean thing!" she says firmly.

Ed smiles. "Good. I believe you. But Tom says that you guys had it in for the new girl from the first moment she came on campus."

"No, that's not true," Lena protests. "She's the one who started it. She . . ."

Lena stops short. Because what exactly *did* Yumiko start doing? I think back. I remember Tom coming into our room to tell us how pretty she was. I remember when she first came into the cafeteria, and everyone looked over at her, and then Zach and Luke welcomed her like they would any new student. And, when she beat me fair and square at wushu, she held out her hand. Then I got angry because Tom thought her drawings were as good as mine. The truth is, thinking back on it, I can't remember a single bad thing she did.

"She's the one who started . . ." Lena repeats, probably doing the same thing. Searching her memory for something bad to report about Yumiko and coming up with nothing.

"She's a spy for Nakamura!" Vic says triumphantly.

Ed looks doubtful. "Oh, really? And how do you know that?"

Vic tells him what we saw—the scene with the envelope and the one at Nakamura's room last night.

He looks even more doubtful. "I don't see how that proves anything," he says after a pause.

I start to think about it too. And I have to admit that I agree with him . . .

"I realize that it's mysterious," Ed says. "But I think you've drawn some pretty hasty conclusions. There are probably dozens of ways to explain all that."

Lena, Vic, and I look at him. Then it hits us. Ed is right. We just got carried away and went way too far. Each of us found different reasons to dislike Yumiko even before we got to know her.

Tom was right, too. This time, we weren't much better than Kim and her clique.

"Right now, there are two important things to take care of," Ed says. "First, you've got to patch things up with Tom. He read your note and he's ready to be friends again. Even before, he wanted to believe you could never have done this. The idea that you might have anything to do with this crazy plan made him pretty upset though. Next thing, we have to get together and to find out who is responsible for the stupid green-dye prank."

As we talk, Vic is writing a note to pass over to Tom. This is what she writes: *Tom, forgive us. Vic.*

I sign my name before handing it to Lena who does the same. She wads up the paper and throws it over to Tom.

Tom opens it without looking our way, reads it, and looks over at us, beaming.

Finally, it's noon Wednesday. We don't have classes because the teachers are meeting for the entire afternoon. We had planned to go to the movies or do something fun off campus, but now all fun activities are off! Mrs. Berrens has forbidden us to leave campus until the guilty one is found.

Still, we agree that Ed is right. The Groove Team is back together, and nothing will stop us from solving this mystery!

We didn't see Yumiko in the cafeteria. Actually, no one seems to know where she is. It's after lunch and we've taken refuge in the editing room where we

85

publish *Groove Zine*. The room is really just a little storage room in the library. Miss Genet, our cool librarian, lets us use it.

We've already discovered a hot clue. A little while earlier in the cafeteria, Lena was standing behind Angie in line. When Angie picked up her tray, Lena noticed that her nails were stained with green . . .

"That's what we'll start with. We're bound to discover more clues," Vic says.

Lena says, "Sure. But remember, we're going to have to come up with ironclad proof. Otherwise, it's useless."

"Yes, but what exactly can the proof be?" Tom asks.

I have a good hunch. "If they used dye, we should be able to find the packaging. It's got to be somewhere around the school."

"Brilliant!" Lena exclaims, getting up. "Come on, let's start looking." Lena always jumps right into action.

"Hey, wait a second. Let's divide up the locations where we have to search," Ed says.

"We have to start with their room!" Lena says. "Vic, Zoe, and I will do that. If you can stand it, guys, start going through the garbage. Let's go, girls!"

Lena is already halfway out the door. She definitely has a plan. And Vic and I are right behind her. "See you later, guys!"

"Wait, Lena! How are we going to get into Kim's room?" Vic asks.

Lena shrugs. "I don't have a clue. I thought you'd have some idea . . ."

I shake my head. This isn't going to be so easy after all. And then, I snap my fingers! I have a great idea. I get out my cell phone.

"Hello! Please give me the number of the Japanese restaurant on Spring Street. I think it's called Karott Sushi."

Before you know it, the delivery has arrived. We have ordered ten sushi platters. It'll be expensive, but worth it—if my plan works.

My mother always says, "You catch more flies with honey." We all know that Kim simply adores sushi. She's up for eating it any time of the day or night. And that's how we're going to trap her.

We tiptoe down the hall and place the package right in front of Kim's door. Vic and Lena flatten themselves against the wall on either side of the door. I knock three times and dash over to the wall on the other side of Vic.

Nothing happens.

"They must not have heard it. We have to knock again," Vic mutters.

I can feel my heart beating hard. I'm sure it's louder than the drums in a rock band. I'm about to go back and knock again, when . . .

The door opens! We hear Clarisse's voice.

"Hey, what's this package doing here?"

Then Kim's voice. "A package? What kind of package?"

"Well it's a big paper bag," Clarisse says. "I recognize this name. It's from the restaurant where we pick up your sushi . . ."

"Sushi!" Kim squeals.

We hear her get up and run to the door. She pushes Clarisse aside and reaches down with both hands toward the bag on the floor. At this moment, we make our move. In a flash, Vic, Lena, and I lunge at Kim and rush into the room. We don't quite make it over the bag of sushi and hear a Styrofoam box crunching under our feet, but that doesn't bother us.

Of course, Kim screams, "My sushi!"

I close the door. Lena tells Kim we think she's behind the green-dye prank. Vic keeps an eye on Angie and Clarisse. (That's an easy job. They are such followers that they don't even think of doing anything without an order from their leader!)

Angie and Clarisse just sit down in their desk chairs and don't make a peep. They watch to see what Kim will say.

Meanwhile, Kim is still shrieking. Lena tells her to

stop yelling.

"Stop worrying about spilled sushi," Lena shouts. "Vic, it's time to find out if there's any evidence here."

Suddenly, Kim is quiet. She looks nervous. And, is it my imagination, or does she look guilty? Does she have something to hide?

Now it's my turn. Let's hope we're on the right track! I open the door to their bathroom and look in the trash basket.

Right on, as Lena would say. Boxes of dye are right in front of me—all green! I come out of the bathroom, waving the boxes over my head like trophies.

"There we go! We've got the proof we need!" Vic shouts.

Kim bursts out, "I knew absolutely nothing about those boxes. It was Angie and Clarisse who cooked up this prank! I tried to stop them, but they just wouldn't listen. I . . ."

"Quit making up stories," Lena says. "I refuse to listen to any more of your lies."

Vic takes the boxes from me, shakes them, and waves them right in front of Angie and Clarisse's faces. Then she does the same to Kim.

"We have a proposition for you," she says. "It's very simple. Either you turn yourselves in to Mrs. Berrens so she can stop punishing the whole class,

or we'll have to take you to her ourselves."

Silence. Kim gives Vic a dark look.

Vic sits down in front of her and smiles sweetly, "I don't care. I've got all the time in the world. But don't expect to eat any of that sushi while you're deciding."

Kim is so mad she's red in the face. Clarisse and Angie look terrified.

"So, what's your decision going to be?" Lena asks, stepping even closer to Kim.

"Okay, okay, we'll turn ourselves in," Kim mutters, at last.

"Bravo!" Vic exclaims. "We'll take you as far as the admin hall, to make sure you don't lose your way! And of course, we're keeping the proof!"

Chapter 9

Apologies

Mission accomplished. We stopped following the three pests only after seeing them knock on Mrs. Berrens's door. And before they went in, Vic stayed in sight across the hall, holding up the empty packages of green dye. It was her way of warning them to tell Mrs. Berrens the whole truth.

Lena called Ed on her cell phone to tell him the news and ask him to meet us in the cafeteria.

Ed and Tom are there, drinking water and soda. Yumiko is with them. Her hands and face are almost back to their normal color, but she still has a scarf around her head. We sit down without saying anything. Yumiko looks at us and softly says, "Thank you."

She's the one thanking us after everything we put her through . . .

"Don't thank us," Vic says. "We realize now that we weren't nice to you at all. We acted awful. We should apologize."

Tom looks very happy. He's looking at Vic with wonder and devotion. That's it! She's regained her diva status.

"I think we were just . . . jealous," Lena says.

Yumiko smiles. "Okay, I admit it, I wasn't totally blameless. When you snubbed me, I tried to teach you a lesson. It wasn't just an accident that I talked to Zach in front of Lena."

Lena blushes bright red.

"Actually, Luke and Zach didn't tell me that they were practicing for the capoeira competition. I just

overheard them talking about it. Zach was planning to surprise Lena. In the end, I spoiled everything. I'm really sorry, Lena."

Lena's face lights up. All that matters to her is that Zach was thinking about her and planning to surprise her.

Then Yumiko turns to me. "As for you, Zoe, I'm sorry about the wushu incident. As I told the teacher, I've been practicing it for a very long time. I knocked you down on purpose."

I shrug. "Hey, it's all right. Anyway, you had a good reason to want to teach one of us a lesson. We acted snobby and mean."

"No you didn't!" Yumiko says. "Actually, I thought your group looked really cool from the start. I hoped I could . . . you know . . . make you accept me. I couldn't really understand why you kept rejecting me. Then Kim was right there in front of me, saying she was the most popular girl in school, and inviting me to be part of her group. That is, if I wanted to. But I could see how she was treating Angie and Clarisse, and that wasn't my idea of friendship. On top of that, she started telling me all these horror stories about all of you, so I told her to get lost."

"Which explains the green hair!" Tom exclaimed. "She had to get back at you."

So now we understand everything. Or almost everything. I'm dying to ask one more question. "There's one little thing I don't get, Yumiko. What was that envelope that you gave to Nakamura the Eel, and what about the argument you had with her?"

Yumiko looks shocked. "You call her Nakamura the Eel?"

Oops. Maybe I shouldn't have said that. Yumiko lets out a big sigh.

"How did you know about the letter and the argument?"

Lena coughs. She's a little embarrassed. "Well, it's just that . . . we spied on you a little."

Yumiko nods her head. "Now I understand. I guess I'll have to tell you everything. Yuko, I mean, Miss Nakamura . . . uh, I mean . . . she's my aunt."

"What?" I'm completely stunned.

"It's true." Yumiko continues. "She's my mother's older sister. They lost their parents when they were very young and it was Yuko, my aunt, who really raised my mother. Both sisters wanted to become dancers and both were accepted into a dance school, but only my mother passed the final audition. Today, she is a principal dancer in the Kyoto Opera. My aunt has been angry with my mother ever since. They haven't spoken in years."

Miss Nakamura wanted to be a dancer . . . That explains why she works here. And that explains the look of joy on her face the day she watched our rehearsal, and the two times I have seen her dancing in front of the mirror.

But there's more to Yumiko's story. "I came to Groove High to get to know my aunt. The envelope I gave her contained a letter from my mother. But my aunt didn't take it well . . ."

"Maybe she just needs a little time," Lena suggests. "Maybe in a couple of weeks, she'll change her mind."

Tom speaks up. "But Yumiko can't wait a couple of weeks. She's leaving in a few days."

Yumiko nods.

"Yes, I applied to two schools, Groove High and another one. Groove High accepted me first and I jumped at the chance to see my aunt. But since then, I've heard from the school in Kyoto. It's the school where my mother and my aunt had their dance training."

"So what . . ." Vic starts, but she's interrupted by Jeremy, who bursts into the cafeteria.

"Oh, there you are!" he says. "I've been looking for you everywhere! I'm here to announce that the first-year students are no longer grounded. The guilty ones have turned themselves in. If you want, you can spend the afternoon off campus!"

"Hooray!" we all shout at once.

It is so great to have the Groove Team back together. And to tell the truth, I'm sorry Yumiko is leaving. She would have been a great new member!

But for now, I want to have a heart-to-heart talk with Ed.

It's fantastic that he's back at school and I really

missed him, but I still want to know why he came back early. I have a strong hunch that it's for a not-so-good reason . . .

GROOVE

zine ★

Edited

by the Groove Team

What a busy week at Groove High.
You probably noticed the temporary
absence from the courtyard and
cafeteria of two students who usually
do not go unnoticed! As we now know,
it was because they were practicing for
a wonderful demonstration
of capoeira which we all
got to see yesterday!
Congratulations, Zach!
Bravo, Luke! You are super
talented!

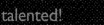

School News

Getting to Know ...
A Brief Visit to Groove High

You may have had the opportunity this week to meet Yumiko Hyori. No doubt you had a chance to appreciate her diverse talents. She was equally good at dance, martial arts, and drawing! Unfortunately, Yumiko has left us to go to another school. Despite some inconvenience she may have undergone during her (too) short stay, she assured us she would remember all of us fondly and treasure the memories of her visit. But not to worry, she gave us her new address so we can stay in touch!

by Zoe

Latest Trends

Japanese Accessories

Perhaps you don't know it yet, but Yumiko Hyori, who spent this last week with us, is going to live in Kyoto. I am interested in the height of fashion in Japan. All those who read manga already have an idea of the great styles and accessories. Leggings are a staple accessory. Special, very thick leggings to be worn with a long, baggy top or under a miniskirt. Barrettes are a popular accessory in Japan, too. Decorative barrettes are used to adorn hairstyles—ladybugs, pompoms, multicolored birds, small dragons, etc. Another popular accessory is the white short-sleeved shirt, worn with a little black sweater with a short v-neck. So, go ahead, and add a Japanese flair to your wardrobe!

by Vic

Sports Page

Martial Arts on the Brain

First, a big hello to our stars: Zach and Luke, who worked wonders last week during the demonstration of capoeira! What skill! What talent! But I would also like to mention the Wushu tournament involving our teacher, Mr. Tian, which will be coming up at the end of the month (which is very soon). You should know that wushu is perfect for learning to control our energy. I invite you all to come and support our teacher. Some of the greatest champions of wushu (Mr. Tian himself a double world champion) will be involved, so the tournament is guaranteed to be a spectacular display of martial arts talent!

by Lena

Japanese Grooves

I took advantage of Yumiko's visit to ask what some Japanese teens are listening to. Here is what she said:

1) 'Hana' is a magnificent song that made its singer Kina Shokitchi, a true star in Asia

2) Kimiko, already popular at only 13 years old, always dresses like a warrior manga!

3) And finally, Nobuko Matsumiya who sings songs that are close to traditional music, is a popular performer.

★ ★ ★

by Tom

CINEMA

Japan's Kings of Animation!

When talking about Japanese cinema, it is impossible not to mention Miyazaki. You may have heard of his powerful imagination and creativity. To check it out, you might want to try some films in this genre: My Neighbor Totoro, Spirited Away, Princesse Mononoke, and Howl's Moving Castle. In another genre, do not miss out on Final Fantasy—the 7 is a gem—and Full Metal Alchemist and Samurai Champloo are noteworthy series, too!

by Ed

HOROSCOPE by Zoe

Aries
Seeking recognition? In working with others, you will find your happiness.

Taurus
It is high time to break into action. You are a little passive lately. Propose projects or field trips, and your friends will be delighted.

Gemini
You must make concessions. Sometimes the advice that you give is good. But you don't have to shine every time!

Cancer
This is no time to relax your vigilance. A single mistake could derail what you've worked hard for.

Leo
Do not interpret too much evidence that seems obvious. Appearances are often misleading.

Virgo
Do you have a feeling you've done something wrong? Can't figure it out? If you can remember, it may serve as a lesson.

Libra
Your heart beats very hard when you hear a certain name spoken. The stars advise you to let them go.

Scorpio
You feel that nothing works for you. Look in a mirror and you might notice that you need to adjust your attitude if you want to earn some sympathy.

Sagittarius
Ah! The family business is very complicated. But do not be discouraged! Time is on your side . . .

Capricorn
Take care of you and only you for a few days. Then everything will be better and you can resume your normal pace.

Aquarius
You showed courage and great judgment. Remember, good deeds are rewarded. You may yet achieve your most cherished dreams.

Pisces
Despite being very busy this week, you have nevertheless continued to think about a certain person. It might be time to tell them!

Our School

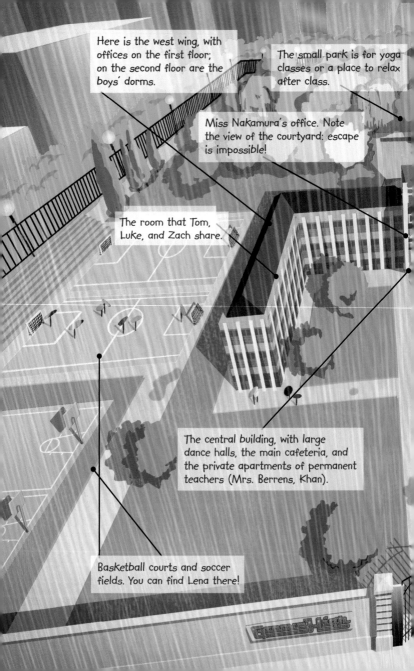

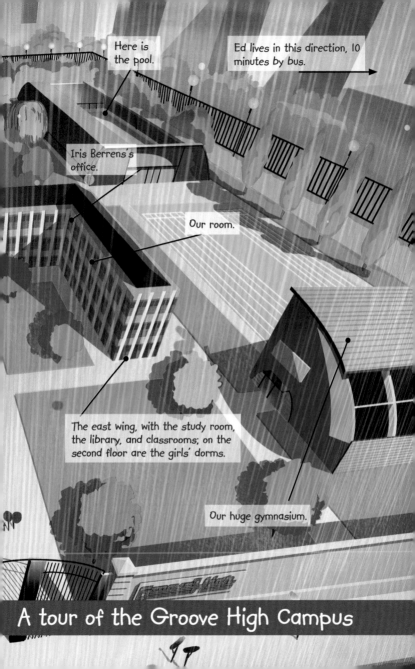

Our Dorm Room

Fashionably designed, well-lit, and well thought-out! Here's a small tour of the room . . .

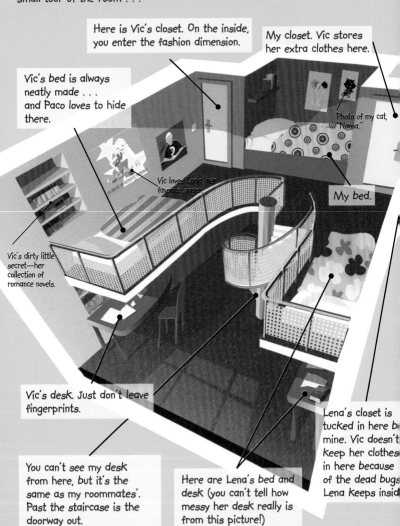

Here is Vic's closet. On the inside, you enter the fashion dimension.

My closet. Vic stores her extra clothes here.

Vic's bed is always neatly made . . . and Paco loves to hide there.

Photo of my cat, "Nama."

Vic loves Lorrie, her favorite singer.

My bed.

Vic's dirty little secret—her collection of romance novels.

Vic's desk. Just don't leave fingerprints.

Lena's closet is tucked in here by mine. Vic doesn't keep her clothes in here because of the dead bugs Lena keeps inside

You can't see my desk from here, but it's the same as my roommates'. Past the staircase is the doorway out.

Here are Lena's bed and desk (you can't tell how messy her desk really is from this picture!)

Here's a view of the lower level of our room, under the loft.

The door. Only Tom doesn't quite understand that you're supposed to knock before you come in.

My beloved heater. I love him so much, I even gave him a name: Raymond. (Don't ask me where that name came from.)

Here's my desk, which you couldn't see before. It is strategically placed near the heater, because I'm like Paco — always cold!

We each have our own sink in the bathroom, which makes it easy to get ready together. Vic has a tendency to invade my territory and Lena's.

Very practical: Our bookshelves are built right into the walls.

The bathroom, where we hide Paco's terrarium when we're in class, under the sinks and behind the clothes hamper. (We use that hamper often, between Lena, who always manages to spill something, and Vic, who changes clothes three times a day!)

When we're in the room, Lena keeps Paco's terrarium on her desk.

The boys' dorm room

The exact same layout as the girls', just with different colors. Personally, I like their room better. What do you think?

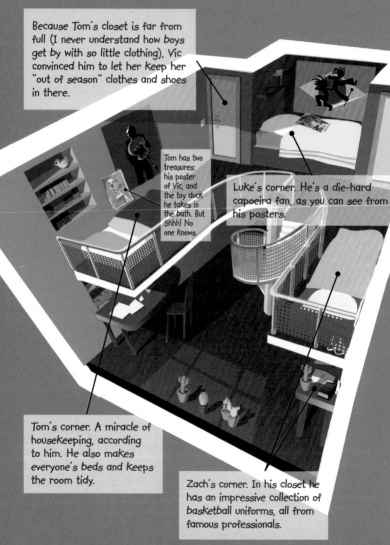

Because Tom's closet is far from full (I never understand how boys get by with so little clothing), Vic convinced him to let her keep her "out of season" clothes and shoes in there.

Tom has two treasures: his poster of Vic, and the toy duck he takes in the bath. But Shhh! No one knows.

Luke's corner. He's a die-hard capoeira fan, as you can see from his posters.

Tom's corner. A miracle of housekeeping, according to him. He also makes everyone's beds and keeps the room tidy.

Zach's corner. In his closet he has an impressive collection of basketball uniforms, all from famous professionals.

Tom and Luke switched desks because Luke doesn't like to be so close to the heater. This boy and I are complete opposites.

Poster of Fernando Yace, the most famous capoeira dancer right now. He is supposed to come to Groove High at the end of the year, and Luke talks about him constantly.

Tom is not a big reader, but check out his awesome music collection!

The bathroom: same as ours. "Wow, for a boys' bathroom, it's pretty clean," Vic says.

Luke's desk. It's in the same place as Vic's, which fills her with joy. She sees it as a sign...

Zach's desk. He's a nature-lover. He takes good care of his plants.

Speaking of hiding places, under the boys' sink are stereo speakers, juice, and snacks for a little party now and then.

About the Author and Illustrator

Amélie Sarn: Amélie has two major flaws: excessive curiosity and a tendency to gorge herself. Not just on food, but on reading, travel, games, children, friends, and anything that makes her laugh. This gives her lots of material for stories! When her publisher asked her to write the stories of Zoe and the Groove Team, she revealed her dark side. Of all the characters in *Groove High*, she admits that her favorite is Kim!

Virgile Trouillot: With his feet on the ground, but his head forever in the clouds, Virgile spent his youth under the constant influence of cartoons, manga, and other comics.

When he's not illustrating *Groove High* Books, Virgile develops animated series for *Planet Nemo*. Virgile spends time in his own version of a city zoo that's right in his apartment. His non-human companions include an army of ninja chinchillas that he has raised himself and many insects that science has not yet identified.

Web Sites

In order to ensure the safety and currency of recommended Internet links, Windmill maintains and updates an online list of sites. To access links to learn more about the *Groove High* characters and their adventures, please go to www.windmillbooks.com/weblinks and select this book's title.

For more great fiction and nonfiction, go to www.windmillbooks.com.